BEN 10™

PERMANENT RETIREMENT
AND SIDE EFFECTS

EGMONT
We bring stories to life

First published in Great Britain 2008
by Egmont UK Limited
239 Kensington High Street
London W8 6SA

Ben 10 and all related characters and elements
are trademarks of and © Cartoon Network.
(s08)

ISBN 978 1 4052 4166 3
3 5 7 9 10 8 6 4

Printed in Italy

BEN 10™

PERMANENT RETIREMENT

BEN TENNYSON IS A 10-YEAR-OLD, ON A ROAD TRIP WITH HIS GRANDPA MAX AND COUSIN, GWEN. THEY'RE TRAVELLING IN AN 'RV' – THE RUSTBUCKET. BEN HAS FOUND A STRANGE-LOOKING WATCH CALLED THE 'OMNITRIX' FROM OUTER SPACE. WITH THE WATCH, BEN CAN TRANSFORM INTO SOME TOUGH ALIEN DUDES. WILL THEY HELP HIM FIGHT OFF SOME BAD GUYS IN THE DESERT?

BEN, GWEN AND GRANDPA MAX ARE DRIVING THROUGH THE DESERT. THEY STOP AT A SERVICE STATION FOR MAX TO TAKE OUT SOME CASH.

AS HE PUTS HIS CARD IN, MAX IS TOSSED ASIDE. A BAD-LOOKING DUDE HAS RIGGED UP A HOOK AND CHAIN TO THE CASH MACHINE. THE OTHER END OF THE CHAIN IS ATTACHED TO A TRUCK!

BEN RUSHES OVER AND PRESSES THE OMNITRIX ON HIS WRIST. HE TRANSFORMS INTO *UPGRADE!* THE GOOD GUY ALIEN THEN MERGES INTO THE TRUCK AND TAKES CONTROL OF IT!

YOUR CASH REQUEST HAS BEEN DENIED!

UPGRADE GRABS THE CHAIN AND FLOORS THE BAD GUYS WITH IT. JOB DONE – THEY'RE POWERLESS AGAINST THIS SUPERHERO!

ONCE EVERYONE IS BACK IN THE RUSTBUCKET, GRANDPA MAX TELLS THEM THAT ISN'T THE END OF THE ADVENTURE!

WE'RE OFF TO SEE YOUR AUNT VERA FOR THE WEEKEND.

BORING OLD AUNT VERA! OH MAN, THIS SUMMER WAS SUPPOSED TO BE ABOUT *FUN!*

"I LIKE AUNT VERA," SAYS GWEN.

DUH, THAT'S BECAUSE YOU ACT LIKE YOU'RE A HUNDRED YEARS OLD!

AUNT VERA LIVES IN A RETIREMENT VILLAGE, BUT IT'S NOT QUITE WHAT BEN EXPECTS. GLANCING OUT THE WINDOW, BEN SEES AN OLD MAN ON THE ROOF OF HIS HOUSE, FIXING A SATELLITE DISH. SUDDENLY HE SLIPS, AND IS ABOUT TO PLUMMET TO THE GROUND WHEN HE DOES A MID-AIR FLIP AND LANDS ON HIS FEET!

WHEN THEY ARRIVE AT VERA'S HOUSE, BEN SPOTS HER OLD NEIGHBOUR, MARTY, LOOKING OUT OF HIS WINDOW. THE MAN GROWLS, CRACKS AND TWISTS HIS NECK, AND SHUTS HIS BLINDS. *WEIRD!*

JUST WATCH YOUR CHEEKS, VERA'S A PINCHER!

GRANDPA MAX'S WARNING COMES TOO LATE AS AUNT VERA PINCHES BEN AND GWEN'S CHEEKS AND GIVES THEM ALL A BIG HUG! "SHEESH", THINKS BEN.

LATER, DINNER IS ANOTHER INTERESTING EXPERIENCE.

"MMM ... DELICIOUS, VERA! BROWN CHUNKS OF MEAT IN JELLY MAKE A TASTY DISH!" SAYS GRANDPA MAX.

AND THE WHITE PARTS ARE CAULIFLOWER!

"EUCH!" SAYS BEN, DROPPING HIS FORK.

"SO, BEN, WHAT HAVE YOU BEEN DOING SO FAR THIS SUMMER?" ASKS AUNT VERA.

"DEALING WITH ALIEN LIFE FORMS," SAYS BEN.

EVEN VERA'S CANDY ISN'T NORMAL!
WHAT SHOULD TASTE SWEET TURNS
OUT TO BE LUMPS OF COFFEE ...

COFFEE!

"*COFFEE!* AS A CANDY?
IS THIS SOME KIND OF
JOKE? I NEED TO USE
THE BATHROOM,"
GASPS BEN.

"IT'S THE ATTACK OF THE
OLD PEOPLE," THINKS BEN.
"I GOTTA GET OUTTA HERE."

BEN DECIDES IT'S
TIME TO GO
GHOSTFREAK!

THERE HAS TO BE SOMETHING FUN TO DO AROUND HERE.

GHOSTFREAK DRIFTS OUTSIDE. ACROSS THE STREET AN OLD WOMAN IS TRYING TO SWAT A FLY IN HER HOUSE. MISSING A COUPLE OF SWATS, SHE HAS A BETTER IDEA. SHE RUNS UP ONE OF THE WALLS, GRABS THE FLY, FLIPS IN THE AIR AND LANDS ON HER FEET. THEN SHE *EATS* IT!

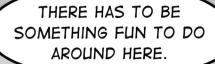

NO WAY! NINJA OLD PEOPLE!

BACK ON THE STREET ...

NEIGHBOUR MARTY SPEEDS BY IN A GOLF BUGGY. IN THE BACK THERE'S A ROLLED-UP CARPET. MARTY STOPS NEAR A LARGE RUBBISH SKIP SURROUNDED BY A GATE. CARRYING THE CARPET, MARTY SLITHERS THROUGH THE GATE WITHOUT OPENING IT!

"THIS PLACE JUST KEEPS GETTING WEIRDER BY THE MINUTE," THINKS GHOSTFREAK.

MARTY OPENS UP A TRAP DOOR BENEATH THE SKIP. SUDDENLY THE OMNITRIX STARTS TO **BLEEP** ... AND BEN IS BACK!

MARTY DROPS THE CARPET AND LUNGES AT BEN. BUT BEN WRIGGLES FREE AND RUNS TOWARDS THE GOLF BUGGY. MARTY CHASES AFTER HIM!

WHAT KIND OF VITAMINS ARE THESE FREAKY OLD PEOPLE TAKING?

BEN SPEEDS OFF, BUT MARTY'S ARMS HAVE STRETCHED LIKE ELASTIC! MARTY PULLS HIMSELF ON TO THE BUGGY, MAKING BEN LOSE CONTROL AND CRASH INTO A WATER SPRINKLER. MARTY'S STRETCHY ARMS SUDDENLY SHOOT BACK INTO HIS BODY, AND HE DISAPPEARS ...

BEN RACES THROUGH AUNT VERA'S FRONT DOOR.

GRANDPA! GWEN!

"SHHHH! AUNT VERA'S IN BED," WHISPERS MAX.

THIS PLACE IS WAY CREEPY! FIRST THIS OLD LADY RUNS UP A WALL. THEN MARTY, THAT WEIRD NEIGHBOUR HAS THESE LONG STICKY ARMS AND THIS BODY THAT OOZED RIGHT THROUGH A GATE ...

OK, SOUNDS LIKE WE SHOULD DO SOME INVESTIGATING ...

BEN, GWEN AND GRANDPA MAX CREEP INTO MARTY'S HOUSE. THEY TAKE A GOOD LOOK AROUND, BUT EVERYTHING LOOKS PRETTY NORMAL. "LET'S CHECK THINGS OUT AGAIN IN THE MORNING," SAYS MAX.

BUT THAT NIGHT, IN AUNT VERA'S BEDROOM, A GLOB OF SOMETHING *STRANGE* CRAWLS ALONG THE FLOOR TOWARDS HER BED. IT SLITHERS ON TO VERA, AND CUPS ITS HAND OVER HER MOUTH SO SHE CANNOT SCREAM ...

BEN AND GWEN HEAD FOR THE RUBBISH SKIP AND THE TRAP DOOR, WHERE MARTY WAS THE NIGHT BEFORE.

THEY PASS TWO OLD WOMEN PLAYING A GAME OF SHUFFLEBOARD. THE WOMEN LOOK UP AND HISS. THEY PICK UP THEIR STICKS AND START BATTING THE HARD ROUND SHUFFLEBOARD PLATES AT BEN AND GWEN! THEY *ZIP* THROUGH THE AIR LIKE MISSILES.

DUCK!

RUN!

BEN AND GWEN DIVE OUT OF THE WAY JUST (AND ONLY JUST) IN TIME! THEY SPRINT ROUND A CORNER AND FIND THEMSELVES CLOSE TO THE RUBBISH SKIP. GRANDPA MAX HEADS TOWARDS THEM.

"GUYS, WHAT'S GOING ON?" SAYS GRANDPA MAX.

THEY'RE EVERYWHERE!

I KNOW, COME HERE, I'LL PROTECT YOU.

AS MAX REACHES OUT HIS ARMS, THEY STRETCH AND S-T-R-E-T-C-H. WITH A HISS, HE CRACKS HIS NECK.

LET'S GET OUT OF HERE!

BEN AND GWEN RUN. BUT THE OLD FOLKS AREN'T GIVING UP. THEIR BODIES HAVE BEEN TAKEN OVER BY *LIMAX* ALIENS!

BEN AND GWEN REACH THE RUBBISH SKIP. "TIME TO GO *WILDMUTT*," BEN DECIDES.

WILDMUTT PUSHES THE RUBBISH SKIP TO ONE SIDE AND OPENS THE TRAP DOOR UNDERNEATH. GWEN LEAPS ON TO WILDMUTT'S BACK AND THEY DROP THROUGH THE TRAP DOOR, AND FALL INTO THE DARKNESS ...

HEY, WILDMUTT, DOES THE EXPRESSION 'LOOK BEFORE YOU LEAP' MEAN ANYTHING TO YOU?

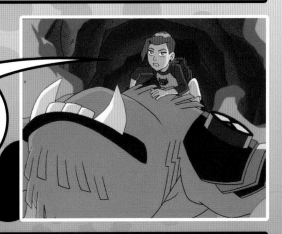

THE OLD FOLKS SLITHER DOWN AFTER THEM ...

WILDMUTT AND GWEN RACE ALONG DARK UNDERGROUND TUNNELS. GRANDPA MAX CATCHES UP WITH THEM BUT WILDMUTT PINS HIM DOWN.

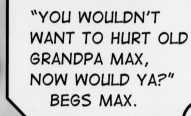

"YOU WOULDN'T WANT TO HURT OLD GRANDPA MAX, NOW WOULD YA?" BEGS MAX.

SUDDENLY, GRANDPA MAX SWINGS AT WILDMUTT AND SENDS HIM FLYING AGAINST THE TUNNEL WALL!

"HEY, SHORT, DUMB AND HAIRY! RULE ONE, HE'S NOT GRANDPA! HE'S AN ALIEN FREAK. AND RULE TWO ... WE KICK ALIEN BUTT!" SAYS GWEN.

WILDMUTT KNOCKS GRANDPA MAX DOWN, THEN STOPS AND SNIFFS THE AIR. HE'S PICKED UP A SCENT! WILDMUTT AND GWEN BOLT DOWN A SIDE TUNNEL.

WHOA!

SLOW DOWN! YOU DON'T COME WITH SEATBELTS, REMEMBER?

UH-OH! THE OMNITRIX STARTS TO BLEEP. WILDMUTT POWERS DOWN BACK INTO BEN.

BEEP!

BEN AND GWEN DISCOVER THAT THE TUNNEL IS FILLED WITH DOZENS OF PODS CONTAINING SLUMBERING OLD PEOPLE!

IT'S LIKE EVERYONE IN THE RETIREMENT VILLAGE HAS BEEN PODDED UP.

ONE OF THE PODS HAS GRANDPA MAX INSIDE!

BEN RIPS IT OPEN AND OUT FALLS A GROGGY GRANDPA MAX. IT'S AS IF HE'S JUST WOKEN UP FROM A DEEP SLEEP.

I WAS OUT FOR A WALK AND THEN ... I CAN'T REMEMBER WHAT HAPPENED NEXT.

WANDERING AROUND, GWEN TOUCHES A STRANGE WALL. IT OPENS UP TO REVEAL THE ENTRANCE TO A **SPACESHIP!** EVERYONE HAS FORGOTTEN ABOUT THE MENACING OLD FOLKS. SUDDENLY THEY SURROUND BEN, GWEN AND GRANDPA MAX. INSIDE THE UNDERGROUND SPACESHIP ARE MORE PODS, AND IN ONE OF THEM IS AUNT VERA!

"TIME TO GO *HEATBLAST!*" SAYS BEN.

YOU GUYS REALLY BURN ME UP, NOW I'M GOING TO RETURN THE FAVOUR!

SOME OF THE LIMAX OLD FOLKS GO FOR HEATBLAST. HE THROWS MASSIVE BLASTS OF FIRE AT THEM. SUDDENLY, ALL THE LIMAXES COME TOGETHER TO FORM ONE HUGE ALIEN!

WHATEVER YOU ARE, YOU JUST MADE A *TERRIBLE* MISTAKE. WE LIMAXES LIVE FOR THE HEAT! WHY DO YOU THINK WE CAME TO THE DESERT IN THE SUMMER?

THE LIMAX GRABS HEATBLAST AND TOSSES HIM THROUGH THE AIR. HE CRASHES AGAINST A WALL BUT GETS RIGHT BACK UP AGAIN.

WITH ALL THE FIGHTING, GWEN'S BACKPACK IS KNOCKED, AND HER WATER GUN FALLS OUT. SOME OTHER LIMAXES SEE THAT THE GUN IS FULL OF WATER AND THEY BACK AWAY. GWEN GRABS THE GUN AND FIRES AT THE LIMAXES. THEY DISSOLVE!

THEY *HATE* WATER! AUNT VERA WHEN SHE WAS IN THE KITCHEN ...

... AND MARTY WHEN I WAS ON THE GOLF BUGGY!

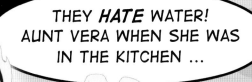

HEATBLAST SPOTS SOME WATER PIPES ON THE CEILING. HE SHOOTS A BLAST OF FIRE AT THE PIPES AND THEY MELT, POURING WATER OVER THE HUGE LIMAX. WITH A FINAL GASP, THE GIANT LIMAX DISSOLVES!

BACK ON THE SPACESHIP, GWEN AND GRANDPA MAX ARE CARRYING THE LAST OF THE PODS AWAY, INCLUDING AUNT VERA'S. ONE LAST LIMAX SLITHERS ON BOARD. THERE'S A HUGE ROAR, AND GWEN AND GRANDPA MAX MAKE IT OUT OF THE SPACESHIP JUST IN TIME AS A DOOR CLOSES BEHIND THEM ...

WHOOSH!

THE SPACESHIP BLASTS UP THROUGH THE GROUND, LEAVING A HUGE CRATER AS IT RISES INTO THE AIR!

HEATBLAST, GWEN AND MAX FIND THEMSELVES IN THE DESERT, SURROUNDED BY ALL THE PODS.

WE SHOULD PUT THEM ALL BACK IN THEIR HOMES SO THEY THINK THEY NEVER LEFT.

GIMME A FEW MINUTES, I'LL SEE IF XLR8 CAN HELP OUT.

ONE BY ONE, THE OLD FOLKS ARE ALL SAFELY BACK IN THEIR OWN HOMES. SOON, IT'S TIME FOR BEN, GWEN AND GRANDPA MAX TO LEAVE.

I'M SORRY BEN IF THERE WASN'T ENOUGH EXCITEMENT HERE FOR YOU. I HOPE YOU WEREN'T BORED TO TEARS.

ACTUALLY ... IT TURNED OUT BETTER THAN I THOUGHT.

BEN, GWEN AND GRANDPA MAX DRIVE AWAY. THEY PASS THE HUGE CRATER, UNAWARE THAT DEEP BENEATH THE GROUND, A PILE OF ROCKS BEGINS TO *OOZE*. IT GROWS BIGGER AND BIGGER AND SLITHERS OFF INTO THE DARKNESS ...

PERMANENT RETIREMENT QUIZ

NOW TEST YOUR KNOWLEDGE OF THIS AWESOME STORY WITH THESE MULTIPLE CHOICE QUESTIONS!

 1 AT THE BEGINNING OF THE STORY, WHERE HAVE MAX, BEN AND GWEN STOPPED OFF?

A) AT A SERVICE STATION
B) AT A SUPERMARKET
C) AT A PICNIC SPOT

 2 WHAT ARE THE VILLAINS TRYING TO STEAL?

A) A GOLD NECKLACE
B) A CASH MACHINE
C) THE OMNITRIX

 3 WHAT'S THE FIRST THING UPGRADE DOES TO STOP THE THIEVES?

A) HE TRIPS THEM UP
B) HE FIRES A LASER AT THEM
C) HE TAKES CONTROL OF THEIR TRUCK

 4 WHAT IS THE NAME OF AUNT VERA'S NEIGHBOUR?

A) MARTY
B) MARK
C) MAX

 5 WHAT DOES AUNT VERA DO WHEN SHE FIRST SEES BEN AND GWEN?

A) SHE INVITES THEM IN
B) SHE SHAKES THEIR HANDS
C) SHE PINCHES THEIR CHEEKS

6 WHAT ALIEN DOES BEN TRANSFORM INTO TO GET OUT OF THE HOUSE?

A) GREY MATTER
B) GHOSTFREAK
C) FOUR ARMS

 7 WHAT IS IN THE BACK OF THE GOLF BUGGY THAT MARTY IS DRIVING?

A) AN OLD SUITCASE
B) A ROLLED-UP CARPET
C) NEWSPAPERS

 8 GWEN HITCHES A RIDE ON ONE OF THE ALIENS. WHICH ONE?

A) HEATBLAST
B) XLR8
C) WILDMUTT

9 WHO REALISES THAT THE LIMAX HATE WATER?

A) GWEN
B) HEATBLAST
C) MAX

 10 WHAT DO THE GANG DRIVE PAST AS THEY LEAVE?

A) A HUGE CRATER
B) A MASSIVE LIMAX
C) VILGAX AND HIS DRONES

ANSWERS: 1-A, 2-B,
3-C, 4-A, 5-C, 6-B,
7-B, 8-C, 9-A, 10-A

ALIEN MATCH

BEN'S SUPERHERO ALIENS EACH HAVE THEIR OWN UNIQUE STRENGTHS. READ THE DESCRIPTIONS BELOW AND DRAW LINES TO MATCH EACH ONE TO THE CORRECT ALIEN.

A

B

C

D

E

1 HUGE AND VERY STRONG

2 ABLE TO FLY

3 LETHAL UNDER WATER

4 INCREDIBLY FAST

5 INTELLIGENT AND TECHNICAL

ANSWER: 1-A, 2-E, 3-B, 4-D, 5-C

WHICH WARLORD?

THESE 6 PICTURES OF THE EVIL VILGAX ALL LOOK THE SAME BUT ONLY 2 ARE IDENTICAL. CAN YOU IDENTIFY THEM?

CODE BREAKER

GREY MATTER HAS INTERCEPTED A CODED MESSAGE FROM VILGAX. USE THE CODE BREAKER BELOW TO READ WHAT IT SAYS.

___ ___ ___   ___ ___ ___ ___ ___ ___ ___ ___   ___ ___
20 8   5   15 13 14 9   20 18 9   24   9   19

___ ___   ___ ___ ___ ___ ___ ___   ___ ___ ___ ___ ___
15 14   16 12 1   14 5   20   5   1   18 20 8

A	B	C	D	E	F	G	H	I	J
1	2	3	4	5	6	7	8	9	10

K	L	M	N	O	P	Q	R	S	T
11	12	13	14	15	16	17	18	19	20

	U	V	W	X	Y	Z		
	21	22	23	24	25	26	27	28

ANSWER: THE MESSAGE IS:
THE OMNITRIX IS ON PLANET EARTH

GOOD OR BAD GUYS?

STUDY THESE AWESOME SILHOUETTES. CAN YOU IDENTIFY EACH CHARACTER? WRITE YOUR ANSWERS ON THE DOTTED LINES. WATCH OUT, THERE MAY BE A VILLAIN ABOUT!

SIDE EFFECTS

BEN, HIS GRANDPA MAX AND COUSIN GWEN
ARE IN THE CITY OF DETROIT. READ ON TO
DISCOVER WHAT HAPPENS WHEN THEY
COME ACROSS A WEIRD GUY WHO WANTS
TO BRING DOWN THE WHOLE CITY ...
CAN BEN'S ALIEN HEROES SAVE THE DAY?

IT'S DAYTIME, IN DOWNTOWN DETROIT. CONSTRUCTION WORKERS HAVE MOVED IN TO DEMOLISH AN APARTMENT BUILDING.

SUDDENLY, A STRANGE FIGURE APPEARS FROM THE RUBBLE. HIS NAME IS CLANCY.

HE GLARES AT THE WORKERS, HIS NARROW EYES GLOWING. THE MEN BEGIN TO PANIC.

GET OUT OF OUR HOUSE!

CLANCY PULLS OPEN HIS COAT AND A SWARM OF *INSECTS* FLIES OUT, ATTACKING THE WORKERS.

I HOPE THIS DOESN'T BUG YOU TOO MUCH!

MEANWHILE, IN THE SAME CITY, GRANDPA MAX AND GWEN ARE MOTORING ALONG IN THE RUSTBUCKET. THEY'RE FOLLOWING A SPEEDING GETAWAY CAR. JUST AHEAD OF THEM IS A SOUPED-UP MOTORBIKE – ONE IMPRESSIVE UPGRADE MACHINE!

UPGRADE SWERVES AROUND CARS LEFT AND RIGHT AS HE GETS CLOSER TO THE GETAWAY CAR.

LOOK OUT! ONE SIDE! COMING THROUGH!

HE FIRES A LASER BEAM AT THE CAR, BLOWING THE BOOT OPEN. OUT FLY TWO HUGE MONEY BAGS.

UPGRADE GETS ALONGSIDE THE CAR. HE POPS OUT THE BIKE'S KICKSTAND, WHICH WORKS LIKE A SHARP DRILL BIT TO CUT RIGHT THROUGH TWO OF THE CAR'S WHEELS. IT CAN'T GO ANYWHERE WITHOUT WHEELS!

THE CAR SPINS WILDLY AND CRASHES TO A HALT. THE THIEF INSIDE GROANS AT THE BIKE WITH NO DRIVER.

WITH THE POLICE ON THEIR WAY, THE UPGRADE
MOTORBIKE DRIVES OVER TO A PARKED ICE-CREAM
VAN. UPGRADE DISLODGES HIMSELF FROM THE
BIKE AND MERGES WITH THE ICE-CREAM VAN,
OOZING INSIDE OF IT!

WELL, I DID JUST
NAB THE BAD GUY ...
NOW WE'RE TALKIN'!

GRANDPA MAX AND GWEN ARRIVE.
"WHERE'S BEN?" ASKS MAX.

"LONG CHASE, HOT DAY ... I'M THINKING ..."
SAYS GWEN, POINTING AT THE ICE-CREAM VAN.

GRANDPA MAX OPENS UP THE ICE-CREAM VAN.
INSIDE, THEY FIND UPGRADE SHIVERING,
SURROUNDED BY A PILE OF ICE-CREAM WRAPPERS!

SUDDENLY THE OMNITRIX BLEEPS, AND IT'S BEN
SITTING THERE, SHIVERING IN THE ICE-CREAM VAN.
HE'S CAUGHT A REALLY BAD COLD!

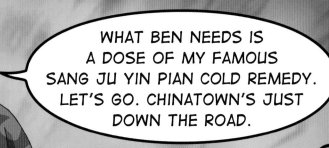

WHAT BEN NEEDS IS A DOSE OF MY FAMOUS SANG JU YIN PIAN COLD REMEDY. LET'S GO. CHINATOWN'S JUST DOWN THE ROAD.

IN CHINATOWN, COUNCILWOMAN JOYCE LIANG IS MAKING A SPEECH. "LADIES AND GENTLEMEN, I WANT TO THANK YOU ALL FOR YOUR SUPPORT OF MY RE-DEVELOPMENT PROGRAMME. IT'S TRULY A DREAM COME TRUE," SHE SAYS.

SUDDENLY THERE'S A LOUD HUMMING NOISE, AND A SWARM OF WASPS DESCENDS. IN THE MIDDLE OF THEM IS CLANCY!

HUMMMMMMM

YOU'RE NOT TEARING DOWN OUR APARTMENT BUILDING, WE WON'T LET YOU.

YOU'RE THE STRANGE GUY WHO WOULDN'T LEAVE. WHAT ARE YOU DOING?

JUST BRINGING YOU HOME FOR DINNER ... YOU'RE THE MAIN COURSE.

THE WASPS SWARM AROUND JOYCE LIANG, COVERING HER.

BEN DECIDES IT'S TIME TO GO *WILDMUTT*, BUT SOMETHING'S WRONG. HE KEEPS CRASHING INTO THINGS. BEN'S COLD IS AFFECTING WILDMUTT'S SENSES! GWEN CLIMBS ON HIS BACK.

OKAY, FURBALL. I'M DRIVING. GO LEFT!

GWEN TRIES TO GUIDE A SNOT-INFESTED WILDMUTT, BUT HE'S OUT OF CONTROL. THEY HEAD BACK TO THE RUSTBUCKET.

MEANWHILE, CLANCY AND THE SWARM OF WASPS HAVE FLOWN OFF, TAKING JOYCE LIANG WITH THEM!

BACK IN THE RUSTBUCKET, BEN'S LAID UP. GRANDPA MAX GIVES HIM A GLASS OF HIS DISGUSTING-LOOKING COLD REMEDY.

IT'S PUTRID STUFF.

IT'S NOT JUST YOU I'M WORRIED ABOUT.

IT SEEMS YOUR COLD HAS SPREAD TO ALL YOUR ALIENS, AS WELL. THERE'S NO TELLING HOW IT'LL AFFECT THEM.

GWEN LOOKS UP FROM HER LAPTOP.

"GOT IT! BUG EYES SAID SOMETHING ABOUT KNOCKING DOWN HIS BUILDING. THE ONLY APARTMENT LEFT FOR DEMOLITION IS AT 8610 CHESTER STREET," SAYS GWEN.

GRANDPA MAX GETS BEHIND THE WHEEL OF THE RUSTBUCKET. THE TEAM IS ON ITS WAY!

AT 8610 CHESTER STREET, INSIDE CLANCY'S APARTMENT, THE COUNCILWOMAN IS TRAPPED. BLACK WIDOW SPIDERS ARE CRAWLING ALL OVER HER.

OUR GRANDFATHER BUILT THIS BUILDING. WE GREW UP HERE, JUST ME AND MY LITTLE FRIENDS.

THE RUSTBUCKET PULLS UP OUTSIDE. GRANDPA MAX AND GWEN TAKE A LOOK AROUND, BEN WANDERS OFF.

THE GANG HEAR JOYCE LIANG SCREAM JUST AS FOUR ARMS APPEARS. GRABBING GRANDPA MAX AND GWEN, HE RUNS UPSTAIRS TO LOOK FOR HER!

FOUR ARMS, GRANDPA MAX AND GWEN SOON FIND JOYCE TRAPPED IN A BUG-INFESTED ROOM.

SUDDENLY, FOUR ARMS DOES A HUGE *SNEEZE*. A DISGUSTING TIDAL WAVE OF SNOT COMES OUT OF HIS MOUTH, BLOWING THE DEADLY SPIDERS OFF JOYCE. SHE IS COVERED IN THE GREEN SLIME - GROSS! BUT JOYCE THANKS FOUR ARMS WITH A WEAK SMILE.

ACHOOO!

DON'T MENTION IT.

CLANCY APPEARS BEHIND EVERYONE, WITH AN ARMY OF BEETLES AND COCKROACHES.

YOU ARE TRESPASSING. WE WILL RULE MANKIND!

AT CLANCY'S COMMAND, A SWARM OF MOSQUITOES *DIVE BOMBS* MAX. HE JUMPS OUT OF THE WAY. GWEN IS CORNERED BY TERMITES THAT ARE EATING THE WOODEN FLOORBOARDS BENEATH HER FEET.

FOUR ARMS IS ATTACKED BY ANTS. HE JUMPS AROUND WILDLY, TRYING TO SHAKE THEM OFF. HE ACCIDENTALLY PUTS HIS LEGS THROUGH WALLS, AND HIS FIST THROUGH THE CEILING.

GRANDPA MAX AND JOYCE PULL GWEN TO SAFETY, NARROWLY DODGING THE FALLING DEBRIS.

YOU'RE DESTROYING OUR HOME!

THE WALLS OF THE APARTMENT CAVE IN, FOLLOWED BY THE CEILING AND THE FLOOR ...

THE WHOLE PLACE IS COMING DOWN!

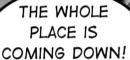

NO TIME!

WE HAVE TO GET OUT OF HERE!

THE HIGH-RISE BUILDING CRUMBLES, THROWING DEBRIS EVERYWHERE.

EVENTUALLY, THE DUST SETTLES. CLANCY BURSTS OUT FROM UNDER A PILE OF BUGS, FOLLOWED BY FOUR ARMS. GRANDPA MAX, GWEN AND JOYCE WERE PROTECTED BY HIS HUGE BODY.

YOU WILL ALL BE SORRY. WE WILL EXTERMINATE THE ENTIRE CITY!

CLANCY IS CARRIED AWAY ON A THICK, BLACK BLANKET OF BUGS ...

WHEN THE TEAM ARRIVES AT THE NUCLEAR POWER PLANT, ALARMS ARE RINGING AND LIGHTS ARE FLASHING. THE DOOR TO THE REACTOR'S CONTROL ROOM HAS BEEN SMASHED OPEN AND THE CONTROLS HAVE BEEN DESTROYED.

CORE TEMPERATURE RISING, APPROACHING CRITICAL ...

CORE TEMPERATURE CRITICAL, MELTDOWN IMMINENT ...

CLANCY ENTERS. HE'S WEARING A PROTECTIVE BODYSUIT – A TOUGH, THICK, DISGUSTING SHELL OF COCKROACHES!

COME FOR A FRONT ROW SEAT? WHEN THE REACTOR GOES SUPER-CRITICAL, I'LL BE AS SNUG AS A BUG IN A RUG!

"OF COURSE. SCIENTISTS THINK COCKROACHES ARE THE ONLY THINGS THAT WOULD SURVIVE A NUCLEAR BLAST!" SHOUTS GWEN.

TIME TO GO *HEATBLAST!*

HEATBLAST APPEARS, BUT THERE'S SOMETHING DIFFERENT ABOUT HIM – THE NORMALLY HOT ALIEN HAS BEN'S COLD ...

YOU GUYS SHUT DOWN THE REACTOR. I'LL TAKE CARE OF BUGSY.

HEATBLAST THROWS HIMSELF AT CLANCY, BUT HE IS **SMACKED** BACK INTO THE WALL.

THAT'S IT. TIME TO TURN UP THE HEATBLAST ROUND HERE!

HEATBLAST AIMS A STREAM OF FLAME TO FRY CLANCY AND THE BUGS, BUT ALL HE CAN MANAGE IS A LITTLE PUFF OF ICY BREATH OUT OF HIS NOSE AS HE SNEEZES ...

MY COLD! IT'S FROZEN MY FLAMES!

GRANDPA MAX AND GWEN HAVE RUN OFF TO FIND THE CORE ACCESS ROOM. THEY FIND HORNETS' NESTS ALL OVER THE CORRIDOR'S WALLS AND CEILING.

UH, OH. REMEMBER THE OLD EXPRESSION 'MEAN AS A HORNET'?

MELTDOWN IN ... **FIVE** MINUTES ...

MAX SPOTS A FIRE EXTINGUISHER. HE HANDS THE NOZZLE TO GWEN AND THEN CRANKS THE WATER ON FULL. GWEN STRUGGLES TO STAY ON HER FEET AS SHE AIMS THE POWERFUL SPRAY AT THE HORNETS, BUT IT WORKS ...

MEANWHILE, BACK IN THE MAIN CONTROL ROOM ...

THE CLANCY BUG MASS IS KICKING HEATBLAST'S BUTT AROUND THE CONTROL ROOM. THE ALIEN HERO TRIES TO FIGHT BACK.

OH MAN, MAYBE WE CAN TALK ABOUT THIS. HEY ...

CHILLY HEATBLAST MAY NOT BE ABLE TO SHOOT FIRE, BUT HE CAN SHOOT *ICE!*

THE CLANCY-BUG MASS LUMBERS TOWARDS HEATBLAST AS THE HERO SHOOTS BLAST AFTER ICY BLAST AT THE VILLAIN ...

CLANCY STARTS FREEZING OVER. HE TRIES TO TAKE ONE LAST, DESPERATE SWIPE AT HEATBLAST, BUT HIS ARM IS FROZEN SOLID.

RESULT! HEATBLAST ADMIRES HIS GIANT ICE SCULPTURE. BUT THE VICTORY MOMENT IS SHORT AND SWEET ...

CORE TEMPERATURE CRITICAL. MELTDOWN IN ... **ONE** MINUTE ...

CORE MELTDOWN IN *TEN ... NINE ... EIGHT ... SEVEN ... SIX ... FIVE ...*

HEATBLAST HAS AN IDEA. HE SHOOTS MORE ICY STREAMS AT THE NUCLEAR REACTOR CORE. THE COOL DOWN SOON STARTS TO WORK AND THE CORE TEMPERATURE BEGINS TO DROP.

... FOUR ... THREE ... TWO ... CORE TEMPERATURE FALLING ... RETURNING TO BELOW CRITICAL LIMITS ...

AWESOME!

HEATBLAST HAS SAVED THE DAY!

BEN, GRANDPA MAX AND GWEN ARE SAFELY BACK IN THE RUSTBUCKET, HEADING AWAY FROM THE NUCLEAR PLANT.

THE BAD GUY'S ON ICE, THE REACTOR'S CHILLIN' ... AND I THINK THAT STEAM KNOCKED OUT THE LAST OF MY COLD.

GWEN SUDDENLY NOTICES A SINGLE COCKROACH EMERGING FROM ONE OF THE CRACKS IN THE RUSTBUCKET. BEFORE SHE CAN CRUSH IT, A HUGE RIVER OF CREEPY CRAWLIES POURS INSIDE ...

WE'VE GOT COMPANY. LOTS OF COMPANY!

MAX PULLS OVER TO THE SIDE OF THE ROAD. AS HE DOES, CLANCY LANDS ON THE RUSTBUCKET, CARRIED IN ON HIS CARPET OF INSECTS ...

WE DIDN'T APPRECIATE THAT COLD SHOULDER YOU GAVE US AT THE POWER PLANT.

BEN TRIES THE OMNITRIX, BUT IT DOESN'T WORK.

HE THINKS FAST. BEN GRABS THE JAR OF HIS SICKLY SWEET COLD REMEDY AND WAVES IT AROUND AT THE MASS OF BUGS. THE INSECTS SWARM TOWARDS THE JAR.

COME AND GET IT!

WHAT'S HAPPENING? *STOP!*

WITHOUT HIS BUG ARMY, CLANCY COWERS IN THE CORNER. GRANDPA MAX APPROACHES HIM AND DELIVERS A POWERFUL *PUNCH*, LAYING THE INSECT DUDE OUT COLD.

BEN TOSSES THE JAR OUT THE DOOR OF THE RUSTBUCKET. ALL THE INSECTS FOLLOW THE BAIT. THEY STREAM OVER A CLIFF AND DOWN TO THE OCEAN FAR, FAR BELOW!

"GOOD. THAT GUY WAS REALLY STARTING TO BUG ME," LAUGHS GWEN.